The Cabbages Are Chasing The Rabbits

Harcourt Brace Jovanovich, Publishers

HBJ

San Diego   New York   London

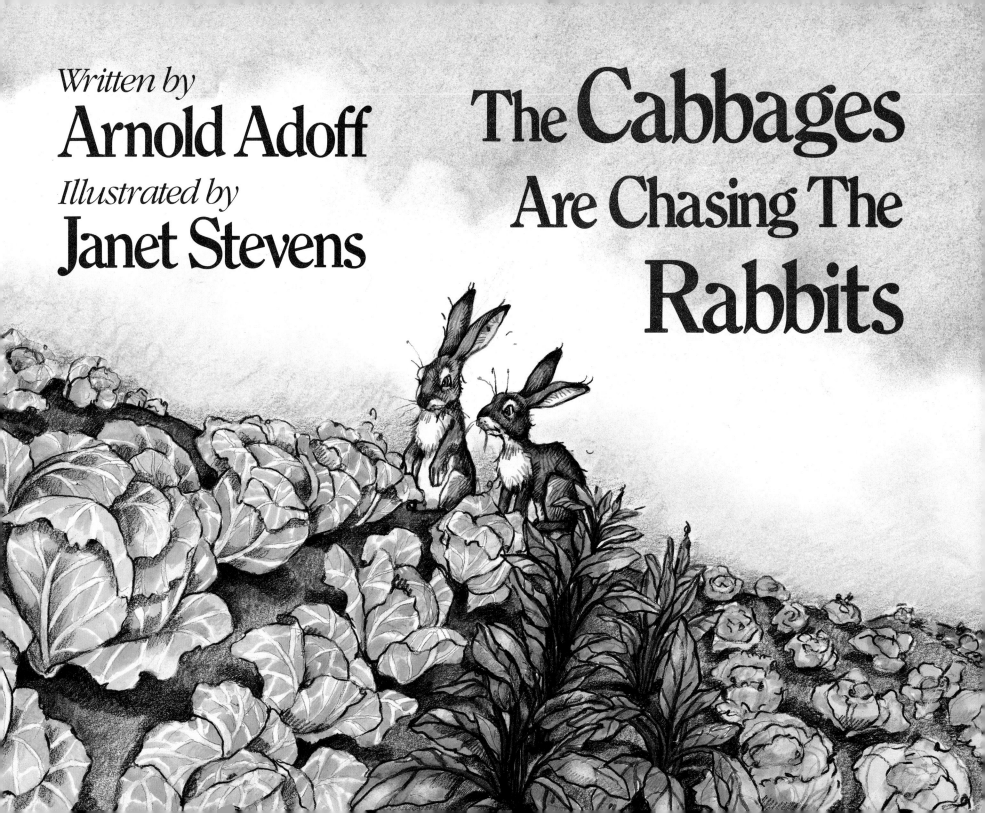

Written by
Arnold Adoff

Illustrated by
Janet Stevens

The Cabbages
Are Chasing The
Rabbits

Library of Congress Cataloging in Publication Data
Adoff, Arnold.
The cabbages are chasing the rabbits.
Summary: A rhythmic cycle of poems about a special
day in May, when the hunter becomes the hunted.
1. Children's poetry, American. [1. American poetry]
I. Stevens, Janet, ill.   II. Title.
PS3551.D66C3 1985   811'.54   85-893
ISBN 0-15-213875-7

Printed in the United States of America
First edition
A B C D E

For All Great Vegetables I Know And Love
—A. A.

For All The Animals
—J. S.

The illustrations in this book were done in watercolors, inks, colored pencils,
and Rembrandt pastels on four-ply Strathmore bristol board.
The text type was set on the Compugraphic 8204 in ITC Garamond Light
by Hillcrest Graphics, San Diego, California.
The display type was photoset in Clearface Bold and ITC Garamond Light Italic
by Thompson Type, San Diego, California.
Color separations were made by Heinz Weber, Inc., Los Angeles, California.
Printed by Holyoke Lithograph Company, Springfield, Massachusetts.
Bound by The Book Press, Brattleboro, Vermont.
Production supervision by Warren Wallerstein.
Designed by Joy Chu.

Once Up
      On A Time

     Or
Twice
Under The First   Tuesday
    In The First Warm
           Week

    In The
       Month Of May

The Sun Comes Out To Stay
And Shines A Good Morning
On A Special
      Kind
Of A Day

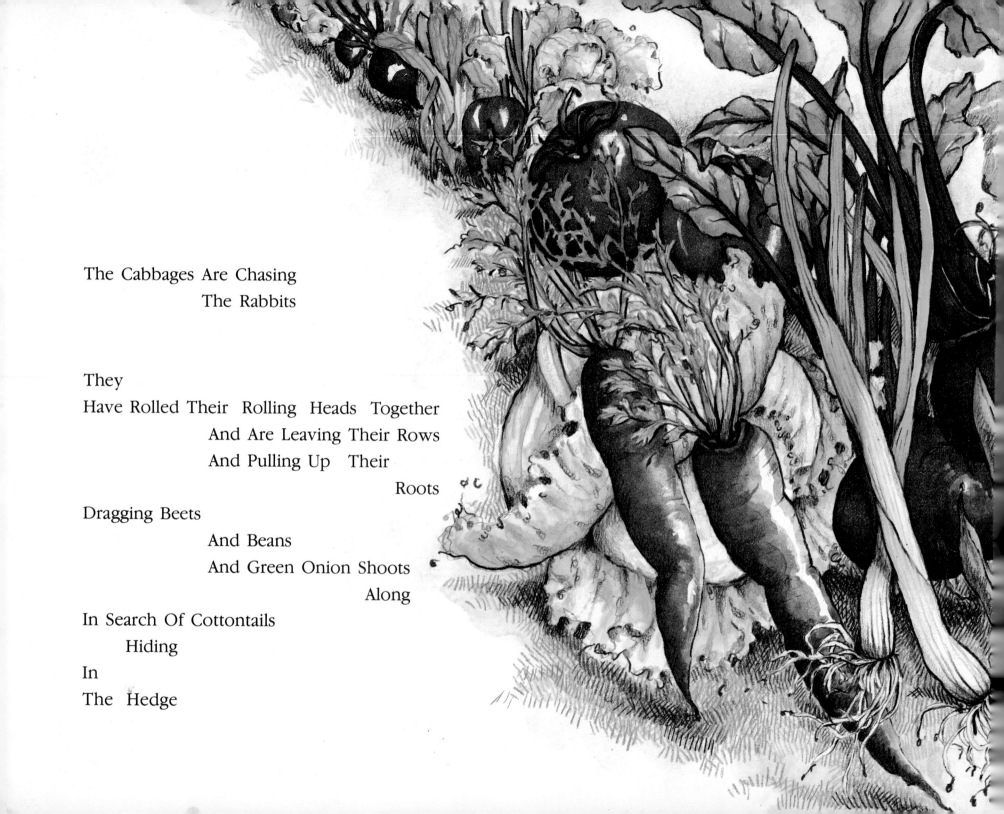

The Cabbages Are Chasing
        The Rabbits

They
Have Rolled Their Rolling Heads Together
        And Are Leaving Their Rows
        And Pulling Up Their
                Roots
Dragging Beets
      And Beans
      And Green Onion Shoots
            Along

In Search Of Cottontails
    Hiding
In
The Hedge

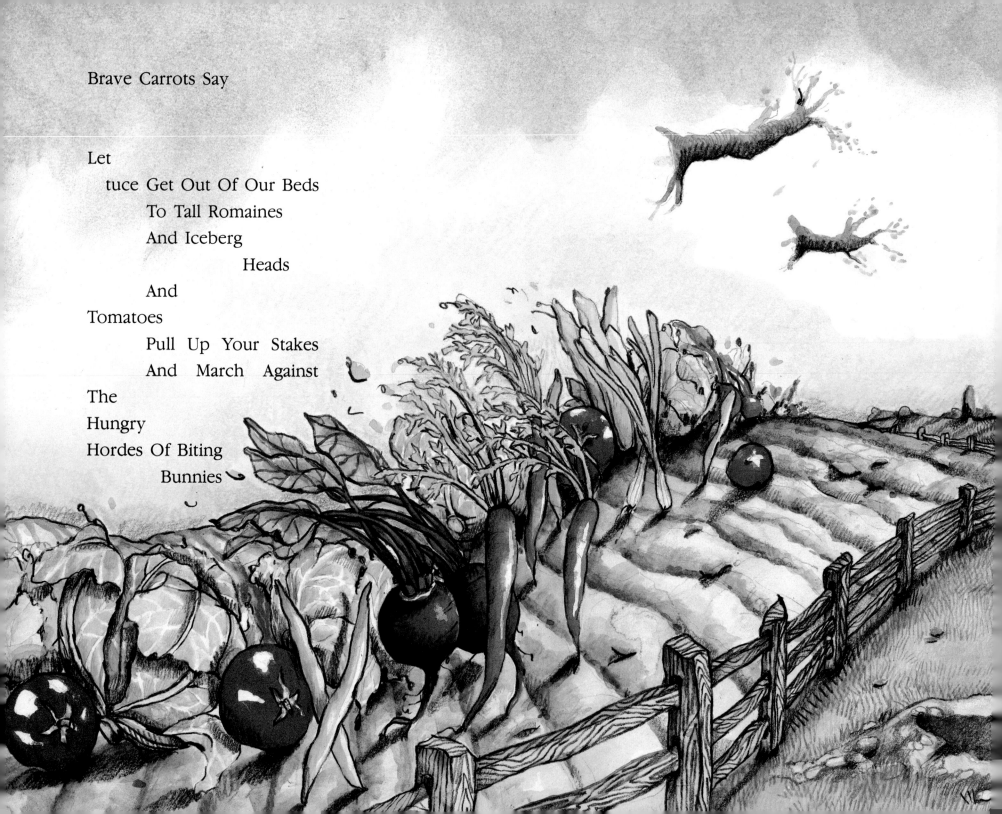

Brave Carrots Say

Let
   tuce Get Out Of Our Beds
      To Tall Romaines
      And Iceberg
           Heads
      And
Tomatoes
      Pull Up Your Stakes
      And March Against
The
Hungry
Hordes Of Biting
      Bunnies

While

The Trees Are Flying Quietly Away
And
The Birds Are Sitting Stubborn On
                                    The
                                  Ground
Waiting For Breakfast To Be Served

Who Ever Heard Of A Patient Bird

Waiting

For Seed Sacks To Open
And Soda Pop
To Pour

Birds Had Better
Hop
And Peck
For
Food

Says The Owl

Then The Sun Comes Out To Stay

And Shines A Good Morning
On
Vegetables
And
Rabbits
And
All Fair Fowl
And
Warms The Wig gling
Worms Of
May

It Was That Kind Of A Special
Kind Of A
Day

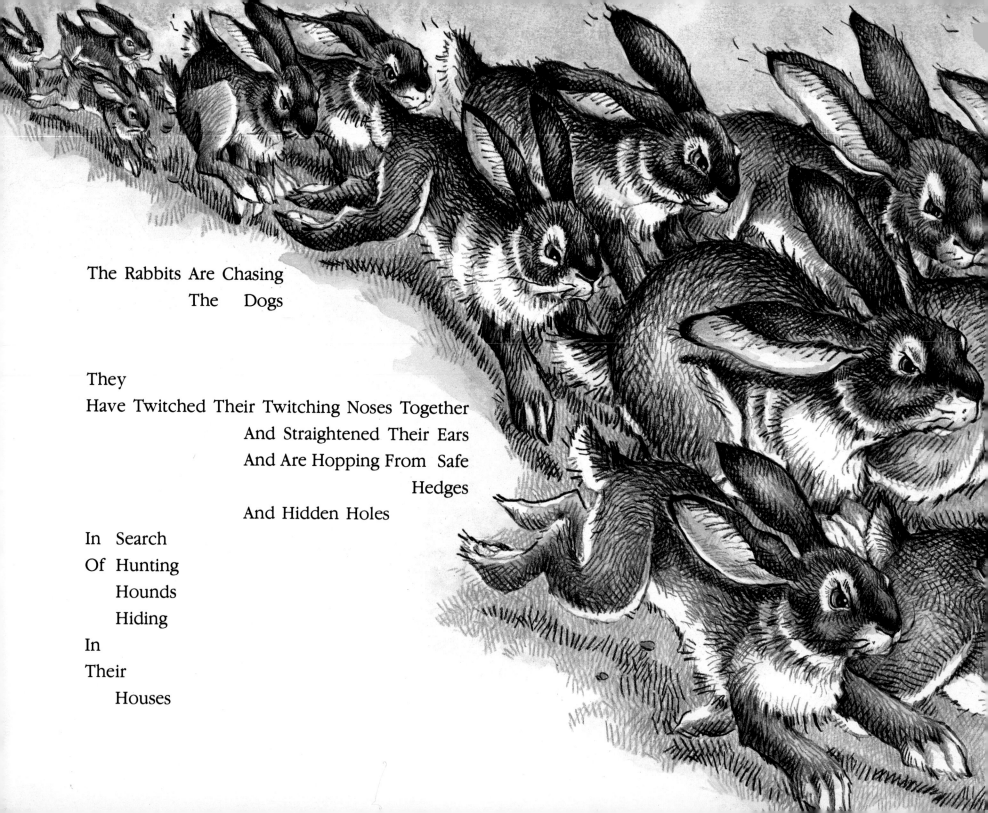

The Rabbits Are Chasing
            The   Dogs

They
Have Twitched Their Twitching Noses Together
                    And Straightened Their Ears
                    And Are Hopping From Safe
                                    Hedges
                    And Hidden Holes
In Search
Of Hunting
    Hounds
    Hiding
In
Their
    Houses

Cottontails Of Courage
Shout

Rabbits Of The Field
Come
Out
And
Together We Can Bite
Back
That
Pack Of Dogs So Mean
The
Way We Bite A Cabbage
Or A Bean

While

The Trees Are Flying Quietly Away
And
The Birds Are Sitting Stubborn On
The
Ground
Waiting For Breakfast To Be Served

Who Ever Heard Of A Stubborn Bird

Patiently
Waiting

For Seed Sacks To Open
And Suet Balls To
Roll
And Bread Crumbs
By The Bowl
And Soda Pop
To Pour

Birds Had Better
Hop
And Hunt
And Peck
For
Food   Says The Owl

Then The Sun Comes Out To Stay

And Shines A Good Morning

On   Vegetables

And   Rabbits

And   Running Dogs

And

All Fair Fowl

            And Warms The Wig

                        gling

            Worms Of

                        May

It Was That Kind Of A
            Special
            Kind Of A
            Day

The Dogs Are Chasing
The Hunters

They
Have Wagged Their   Wagging Tails Together
And Are
Barking
Their   Loudest
Barks

Smelling
For The Smell Of
Gun Powder
In The Forest

In Search
Of Hateful
Hunters
Hiding
Behind
Trees

Careful
Canines

Take Their Paws
Off
Of   Their   Ears
And
      Smile

While

The Trees Are Flying Quietly Away
And
The Birds Are Sitting Stubborn On
                              The
                           Ground
Waiting For Breakfast To Be Served

Who Ever Heard Of A Patient Bird

Stubbornly
Waiting
For Seed Sacks To Open
And Suet Balls To
Roll
And Bread Crumbs
By The Bowl
And Southern Fried Pan Cakes To
Flop
And Soda Pop
To Pour

Birds Had Better
Hop And Hunt And
Stop
And Start To Peck For Food

Says The
Owl

                And Shines A Good Morning
On   Vegetables
And   Rabbits
And   Running Dogs
And   Hateful
            Hunters
And
All   Fair   Fowl
And Warms The
                    Wig
                        gling
        Worms Of
                May

It Was That Kind Of A   Special
                Kind Of A
                        Day

The Hunters Are Chasing
         The Trees

They
Have Pointed Their Pointing Guns Together
     And Piled Them Neatly On The Ground
                    Away From Every Living
                                    Thing

In Search
Of Sweet
         Dreams On A Quiet
                    Afternoon

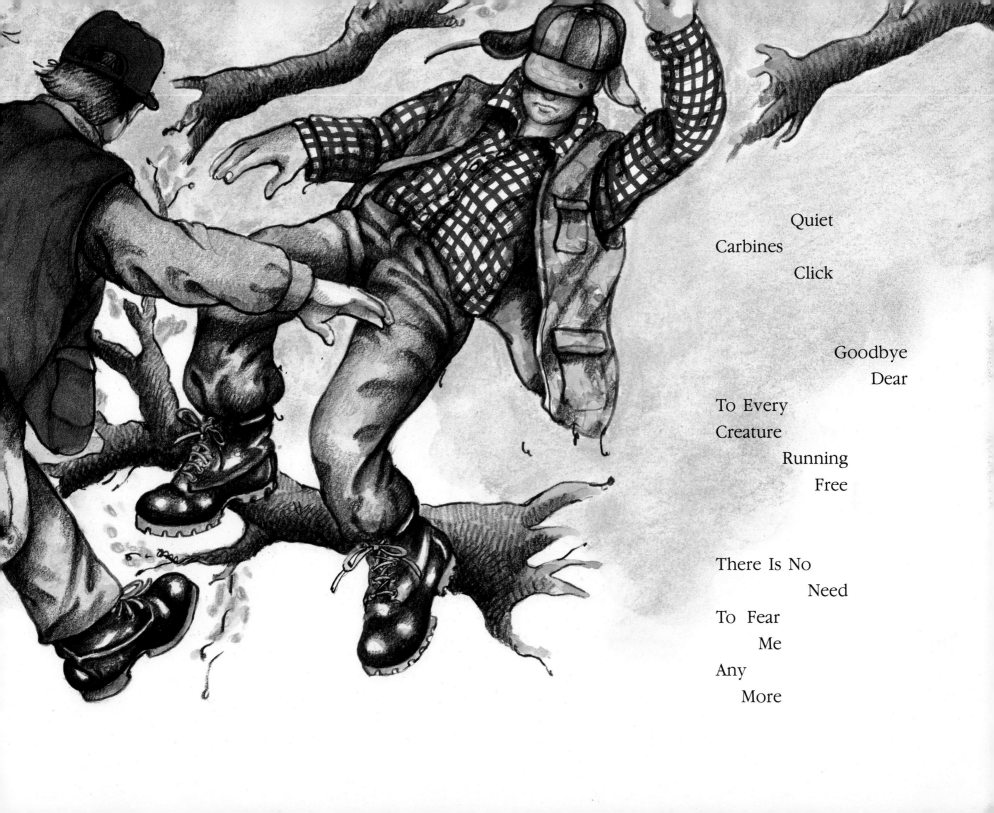

Quiet
Carbines
Click

Goodbye
Dear
To Every
Creature
Running
Free

There Is No
Need
To Fear
Me
Any
More

While

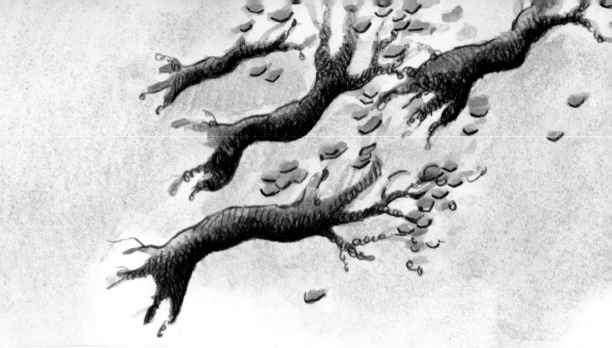

The Trees Are Flying Quietly Away
And
The Birds Are Sitting Stubborn On
                                        The
                                    Ground
Waiting For Breakfast To Be Served

Who Ever Heard Of A Stubborn Bird

Patiently
Waiting
For Seed Sacks To Open
And Suet Balls To
Roll
And Bread Crumbs
By The Bowl
And Southern Fried Pan Cakes To
Flop
And Soda Pop To Pour
And Apples Rotten
To The Core

Birds Had Better
H o p
A n d
H u n t
A n d
Stop
And Start To Peck For Food

Says The Owl

Then The Sun Comes Out To Stay

And Shines A Good Morning
On   Vegetables
And Rabbits
And Running Dogs
And Hateful
        Hunters
And Thick
        Trees
And
All   Fair Fowl
And Warms The W g l n
                    i g i g
        Worms Of
                May

It Was That Kind Of A
                Special
                Kind Of A
                        Day

The Trees Are Chasing
    The Leaves

And
The Leaves
    Are Blowing
In
The Spring Time
    Breeze

In Search
Of Branches
And
    Stubborn
      Hungry
        Birds

The Cabbages Are Chasing The Rabbits

And
The Rabbits   Are Chasing The Dogs
And
The Dogs   Are Chasing The Hunters
And
The Hunters   Are Chasing The Trees
And
The Trees   Are Chasing The Leaves
And
The Leaves   Are Blowing In
                            The Spring
                            Time
                            Breeze
And
The Birds   Are Sitting Stubborn On
                            The
                            Ground
Waiting For Breakfast   To Be Served

Then The Sun Comes Out To Stay

     And Shines A Good Morning

On   Vegetables

And Rabbits

And Running Dogs

And Hateful
       Hunters

And Thick
       Trees

And Lovely
       Leaves

And

All Fair Fowl
     And Warms The
             W i g g l i n g
      Worms Of
        May

Once Up
    On A Time

    Or
Twice
Under The First   Tuesday
   In The First Warm
            Week
   In The
        Month Of May

It Was A Special Kind
    Of A Morning

It Was A Special Kind Of
           A
       Day